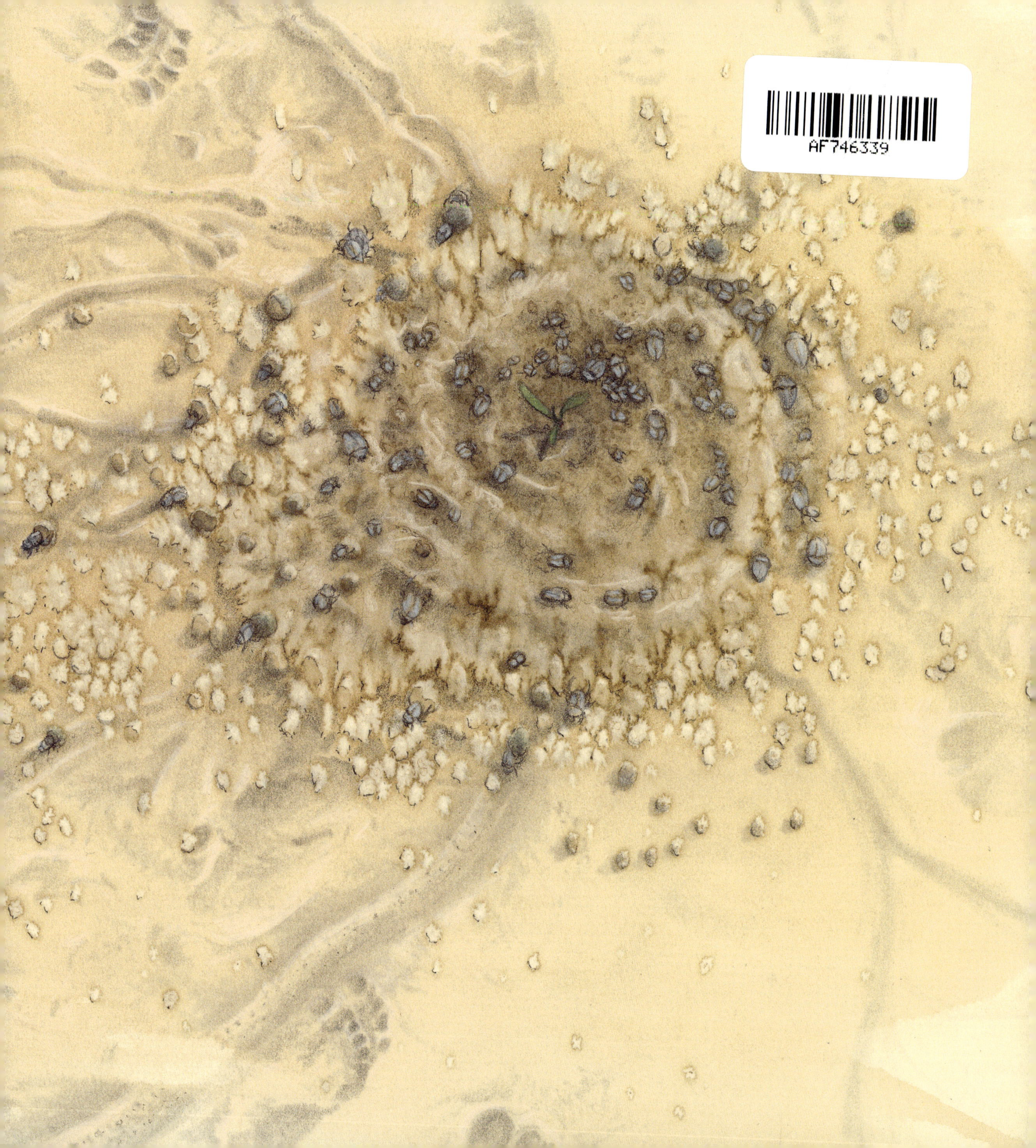

WALKING TOGETHER

Coral Vass Dub Leffler

A Scholastic Press book from Scholastic Australia

For the history makers who fought for equality and for those who continue to work to bring change, we stand by you and walk with you. – CV

This book is for every sole that leaves footprints on this land. – DL

Scholastic Press
An imprint of Scholastic Australia Pty Limited
PO Box 579 Gosford NSW 2250
ABN 11 000 614 577
www.scholastic.com.au

Part of the Scholastic Group
Sydney • Auckland • New York • Toronto • London • Mexico City
New Delhi • Hong Kong • Buenos Aires • Puerto Rico

Published by Scholastic Australia in 2024.

Dub Leffler created these illustrations using watercolour paint and pencil, coffee and salt.

NATIONAL LIBRARY OF AUSTRALIA
A catalogue record for this book is available from the National Library of Australia

ISBN: 978-1-76112-626-0

Typeset in Brandon Grotesque
Book design by Astred Hicks.

Scholastic Press acknowledges the Traditional Owners of Country throughout Australia.
We pay our respects to Elders past and present.

Printed in China by RR Donnelley.
Scholastic Australia's policy, in association with RR Donnelley, is to use papers that are renewable and made efficiently with wood from responsibly managed sources, so as to minimise its environmental footprint.

10 9 8 7 6 5 4 3 24 25 26 27 28 / 2

Communication is the key to understanding and learning.
Deep listening assured. Whispers through the wind carried across
the landscapes bringing all peoples together to share in a great journey
of support for one and all to ensure all voices are heard.
United we are stronger and walking together we can learn and we will grow.

– ***Lee Joachim, Yorta Yorta man***

I heard a call beyond the sea,
I heard it say, 'Come walk with me.'
It echoed out, 'Come hold my hand,'
across this great wide southern land.

It said, 'I've walked the longest road
and carried far, a heavy load.'
But as I listened, I could see
the invite wasn't just for me.

It was a call to everyone . . .

to walk together, ‘Will you come?

Will you walk this final part?

A journey started from the heart?’

The call was heard by only few,
but one by one, it slowly grew.
It rang out through the streets and lanes,
across the mountains and the plains.

From cities to the great outback,
for all Australians, white and black.
I heard the call both far and wide,
to stand together, side by side.

From Cable Beach to Gundagai,
the call grew stronger with each cry.

Up Cradle Mountain in the south
and to the Sydney Opera House.
It travelled out to Kakadu
and down to Cavill Avenue.

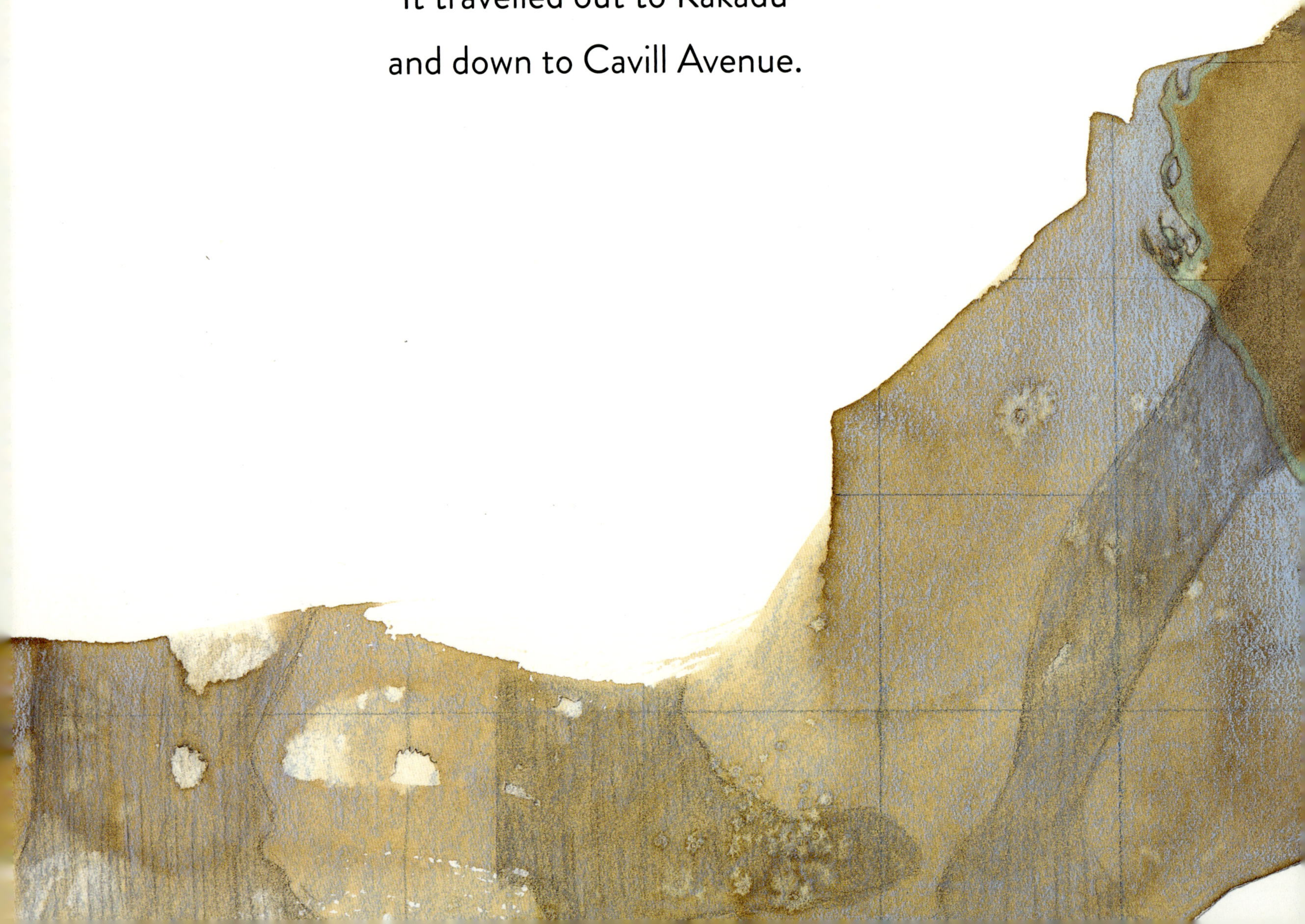

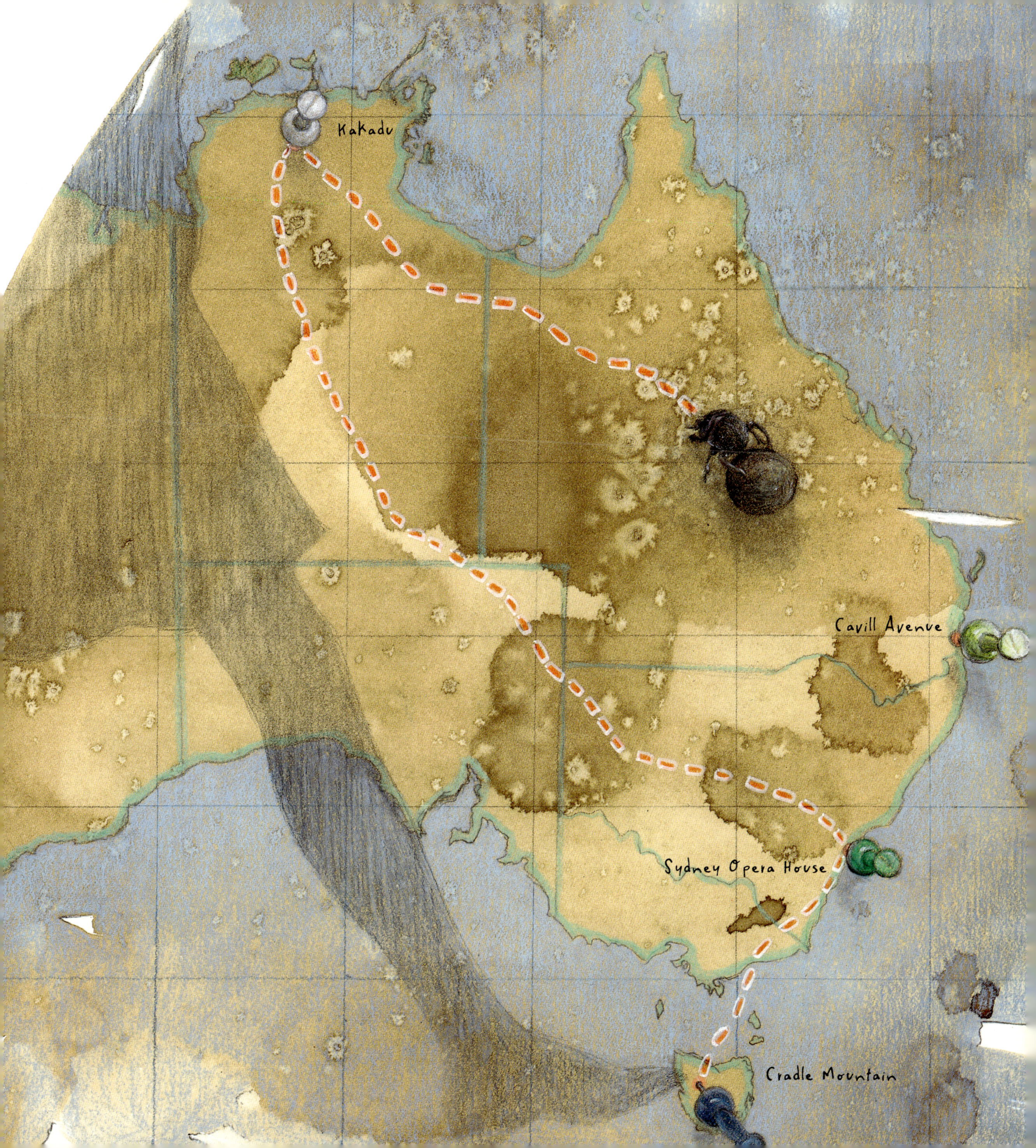
Kakadu
Cavill Avenue
Sydney Opera House
Cradle Mountain

It sounded past the Coral Sea
and over to the Kimberley.

From where the ocean meets the road,
to where the Murray River flowed.

From Ningaloo to Byron Bay,
Mount Isa to Savannah Way.
And high above the West Gate Bridge,
it echoed out to Lightning Ridge.

From busy airports' interchange,
along the Great Dividing Range.

The chorus sang through Arnhem Land,

'Come walk with us and hold our hand.'

To Torres Strait beyond Cape York,
from coast to coast, Australians walked.
From Margaret River to Lake Eyre,
the people came from everywhere.

I saw, throughout this sundrenched land,
people walking hand in hand.
One by one and shore to shore,
Australians trekked, unlike before.
A movement that began and grew . . .

. . . straight from the heart of Uluru.

So, I will come, I'll do my part
and we'll walk together, from the heart.
Step by step, we'll start again.
Side by side, we'll be a friend.

And, so, I'm asking everyone . . .

Will you join us?

Will you come?

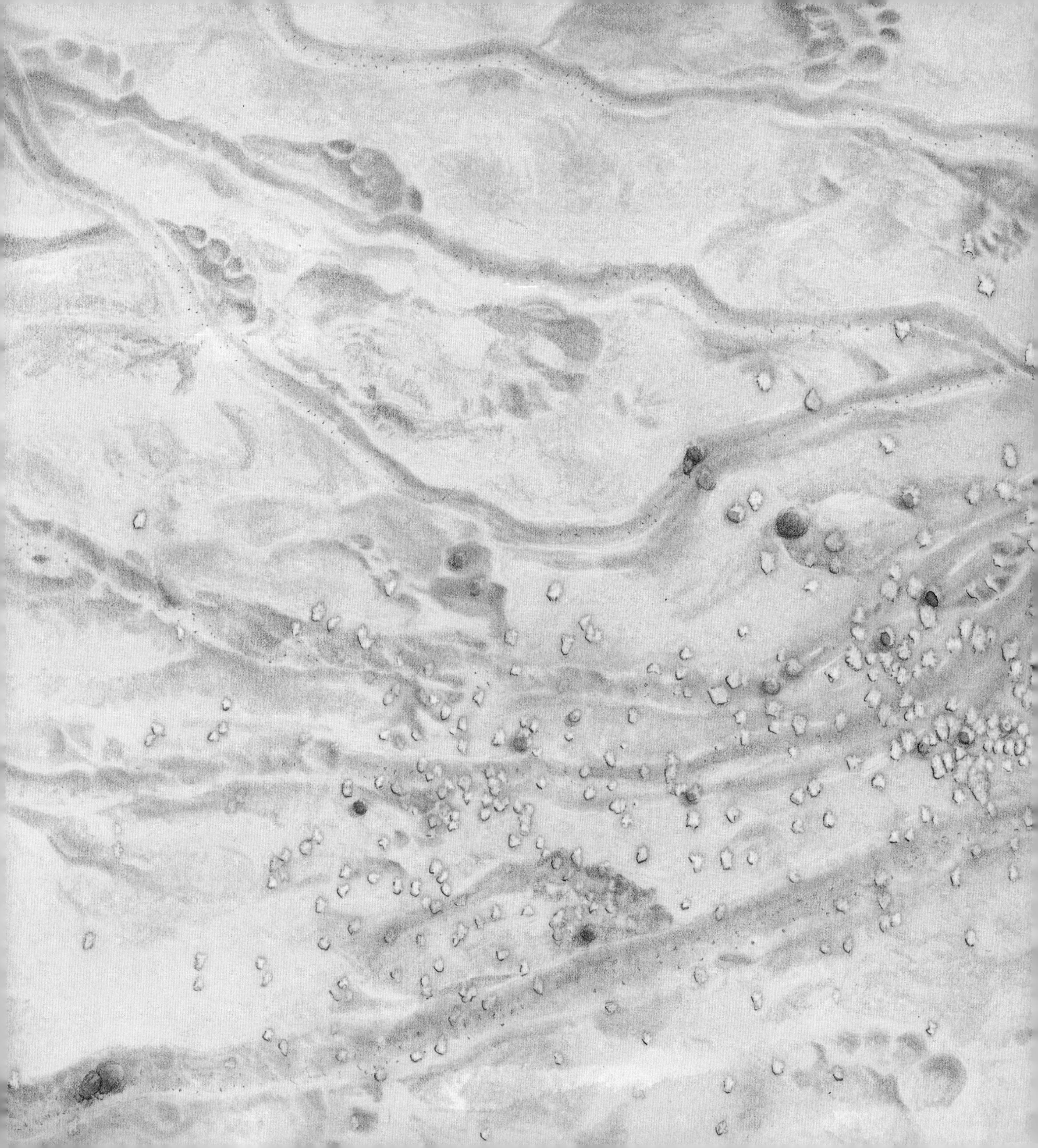